Dougal Strikes A

One day, Mr MacHenry told everyone he had arranged for them to visit a friend of his who had a farm. 'Do you all good, a day in the country,' he said.

'We're *always* in the country,' said Dougal. 'We *live* in the country. How about a trip to London?'

'We can do that another day, Dougal,' said Florence. 'I'd like to go to a farm.'

Dougal sighed. 'I can see trouble ahead,' he said, 'squelching through mud, falling into ditches, being chased by mad bulls . . .'

'Really?!!' said Ermintrude, eagerly.

'I don't want to be chased by a mad bull,' said Brian nervously. 'It might catch me.'

'We should be so lucky,' muttered Dougal.

Dougal Strikes Again

Eric Thompson

Based on stories of The Magic Roundabout *by Serge Danot*

Illustrated by David Barnett

KNIGHT BOOKS
Hodder and Stoughton

Based on the original BBC TV series
The Magic Roundabout
Copyright © 1973 Serge Danot
English text copyright © 1973 Eric
Thompson
Illustrations copyright © 1973
Brockhampton Press Ltd

First published in Great Britain in 1973
by Knight Books

The characters in these stories which
appear in the television films were
originally created by Serge Danot for
ORTF in a series entitled *Le Manège
Enchanté*, and *The Magic Roundabout*

British Library C.I.P.
A catalogue record for this title
is available from the British Library

ISBN 0 340 58157 3

Printed and bound in Great Britain for
Hodder and Stoughton Paperbacks,
a division of Hodder and Stoughton
Ltd., Mill Road, Dunton Green, Seven-
oaks, Kent TN13 2YA. (Editorial
Office: 47 Bedford Square, London
WC1B 3DP) by Cox & Wyman Ltd.,
Reading.

CONTENTS

Ermintrude to the rescue

Dougal had just finished his fourth slice of toast and marmalade and was just starting on his fifth cup of tea, when Brian arrived. Dougal looked at him coldly. Brian sat on a chair and started to hum quietly to himself. It was very quiet, just the clock ticking and Brian humming and the kettle hissing.

'Quiet, isn't it?' said Brian loudly.

Dougal choked on his tea and spluttered. 'Of all the great oafs I have ever encountered,' he said, 'you are without doubt the greatest.'

'What have I done?' said Brian innocently.

'*Done?!*' said Dougal. 'Done!!? You have upset my morning. You have disturbed my routine. You have entered uninvited and YOU HAVE MADE MY TEA GO UP MY NOSE !!!'

'In that case I am very contrite,' said Brian, 'but it *is* half past eleven.'

'What's that got to do with it?' said Dougal.

'And it's Tuesday,' said Brian significantly.

'You said that significantly,' said Dougal. 'What are you getting at, snail?'

'Look, old hairy chum,' said Brian. 'It's half past eleven on a Tuesday and you are

6

sitting here eating toast and drinking tea. What does that suggest to your powerful brain?'

'That it's just an ordinary Tuesday,' said Dougal, pouring himself another cup of tea.

'Work,' said Brian quietly.

Dougal looked at him. 'I beg your pardon?' he said.

'Work,' repeated Brian.

'Work?' said Dougal, still pouring.

'Work,' said Brian. 'And another thing,' he added.

'What?' said Dougal.

'Your teacup's full,' said Brian.

'Eek!!' screeched Dougal, mopping furiously. 'WHY DIDN'T YOU TELL ME?!!'

'I did,' said Brian.

Dougal sat back and sighed. 'I don't know why I let you in here,' he said. 'You're a disruptive influence. But now you're here, I suppose I'd better know what's on your tiny, cloggy mind.'

Brian poured himself a cup of tea. 'Now, I want you to preserve an icy calm,' he said, 'and listen.' He sipped. 'At eleven-thirty on Tuesdays most people in the world are at work. You are *not*. Why not? we ask ourselves. Ah! we say. Why not indeed, we say.'

'Hang on a minute,' said Dougal. 'Who's this "we" you're on about?'

'Well me really,' said Brian, 'but everybody's talking, and the general opinion *is* that you should get a job and keep us all in the manner to which we are accustomed.'

'That's *marvellous!*' said Dougal. '*Marvellous!* I've got to work my patties to the bone to keep the lot of you in rotten idleness.'

'Well, it's not quite as simple as that,' said Brian.

'Simple or not, I won't do it,' said Dougal.

Brian got up. 'Is that your final word?' he

asked, sternly.

'Yes,' said Dougal.

'I shall then convey that to the others,' said Brian. He went to the door. 'Of course, you realize what this means?' he asked.

'Er . . . no,' said Dougal, slightly nervously.

'No matter,' said Brian. 'No matter. Suffice it to say . . .'

'What?' said Dougal.

'*You have been warned,*' said Brian. And he left.

Dougal became very agitated.

'They've obviously got some fiendish plan,' he muttered. 'Work? Work? Don't they realize I'm a gentleman and a dog? Oh, I suppose I'd better go and see what they're up to, the toads. My friends, huh!' And he put on a clean collar and went.

In the garden Dougal's friends were waiting. They had spread a banner between two trees. It read:

Dougal arrived. He looked at them all. Florence smiling; Dylan fast asleep; Ermintrude wearing a large pair of blue dungarees, and Brian sitting in a deckchair.

'Now what *is* all this?' said Dougal.

'I *told* you,' said Brian. 'Work!'

'Sit down, Dougal,' said Florence, 'and we'll explain.' Dougal sat down, sighing heavily. 'We think that one of us should get a job,' Florence went on, 'and when we weighed it all up, the obvious choice seemed to be you.'

'We need money,' said Brian, loudly.

'Sh!!' said Florence.

'So we've sorted out some jobs for you, dear thing,' said Ermintrude. 'And we want you to choose.'

Florence took a piece of paper out of her pocket. 'This is the list of jobs,' she said. 'Ahem. One, Prime Minister. Two, President of the Board of Trade. Three, Archbishop of York. Four, King.'

Dougal was silent.

'Are you qualified for any of those, old chum?' said Brian.

Dougal gave him a withering look. 'Not *fully*,' he said.

'Oh,' said Brian. 'In that case we must consult list two.' And he opened a piece of paper. 'One, rag and bone dog. Two, picker-up of old toffee papers. Three, postman biter. Four, wet blanket drier.' He looked at Dougal.

'Anything there that appeals?' he asked.

Dougal got up. 'Now I don't know what you're all on about,' he said slowly, 'but it's quite obvious to me that you're up to something. Now you know me – I can take a joke . . .' He laughed. 'But I think I should tell you that nothing would persuade me to go to work to KEEP YOU LOT IN IDLENESS ! ! !' He paused. 'Do I make myself clear?'

'But we need some money, dear thing,' said Ermintrude.

'Why?' said Dougal. 'We've never needed money before. Why this sudden rush for money?'

'We've got to buy the garden,' said Florence. Dougal looked at her.

'We've got to *what?*' he asked.

'They're going to build a motorway through us,' squeaked Brian, 'with fly-overs and crossovers and pull-overs and things.'

'Is this true?' said Dougal, faintly.

'Yes,' said Florence. 'So we've got to buy the garden to stop all that happening. You see, apparently we're down in the plans as waste ground.'

'WASTE GROUND!' said Dougal. 'Where I live is waste ground?!! I've never heard of such a thing. We must act! We must do something! We must prepare to repel bulldozers!'

'We are prepared,' said Brian.

'How?' said Dougal.

'You're going to work to earn the money to buy the garden,' said Brian, patiently.

Dougal sat down. 'How much do they want for it?' he groaned.

'Two million pounds,' said Brian.

'WHAT?!' said Dougal. 'How am I going to earn two million pounds? It'll take *weeks*.'

Ermintrude gave a little cough. 'May I make a suggestion, dear dog?' she said.

'Of course you may, Ermintrude,' said Florence.

'She asked *me*,' said Dougal.

'Sorry,' said Florence.

'Well, anyway,' said Ermintrude, 'my suggestion is this. Dear Dougal doesn't seem too keen on the work idea so let's look for buried treasure and when we find some, sell it for two million pounds and there you are . . .'

No one said anything.

'Er . . . that's a great suggestion,' said Brian.

'I knew *you*'d like it,' hissed Dougal.

'Er . . . Ermintrude,' said Florence, 'there is just one thing. I don't think there's a lot of buried treasure around.'

'Oh, I know where there *is* some,' said Ermintrude.

'Then why haven't you dug it up?' said Florence.

'What would I do with treasure?' laughed Ermintrude. 'But it's different now that we *need* it.'

'Well, what are we waiting for?' said Florence, and after waking up Dylan they all rushed off to dig up the buried treasure.

'This is madness,' panted Dougal.

'Bear up, old chum,' said Brian.

They arrived at a little wood and Ermintrude started to dig madly with her horns.

'Do you think she really knows what she's doing?' mused Dougal.

'No,' said Brian.

Ermintrude got deeper and deeper as the

hole she was making got bigger and bigger. The others gathered round the edge to watch.

'Like . . . er . . . where's this treasure at . . . Australia?' murmured Dylan.

'Are you all right, Ermintrude?' shouted Florence, anxiously.

'Fine, dear heart,' boomed Ermintrude from the bottom of the hole. 'Nearly there.'

Suddenly, there was a WHOOSH! Up, out of the hole, shot a jet of black liquid. On top of it, like a cork, was Ermintrude.

'She's struck oil,' said Brian, happily.

'Get me down!' shrieked Ermintrude, black as ink.

'Hold on!' they shouted. 'WE'LL THINK OF SOMETHING!' They all sat down to think.

'It's not going to be easy,' said Brian.

'No,' said Florence.

'I wonder if she . . . like . . . found the treasure,' said Dylan.

Dougal gave a little shriek. He got up and rushed around. 'THAT'S IT!' he screeched. 'THAT'S IT!'

'What's what?' they asked.

'THE TREASURE,' said Dougal. 'Oil! People pay millions and millions of pounds for oil! WE'RE RICH!!'

'But what about Ermintrude?' said Florence. They looked. Ermintrude was still bobbing up and down and looking very unhappy.

'She's posing us a bit of a problem,' said Brian.

But before they could decide what to do about Ermintrude they heard a noise. It was a large van and it came to a stop beside them. Out of it got two men dressed in overalls and caps.

'This looks like it, Francis,' said one.

'Definitely, Patrick,' said the other.

'A proper leak, Francis,' said Patrick.

'Definitely, Patrick,' said Francis. The two men opened the door of the van and got out a large ladder.

'Got your end, Francis?' said Patrick.

'Definitely,' said Francis. They lowered the ladder into the hole and climbed down. Dougal and the others watched and waited. From inside the hole came the noise of clanging and banging and then the jet of oil started to get smaller. Ermintrude gradually came downwards and just as she reached the hole she stepped off. 'My hat's ruined,' she said sadly.

Patrick and Francis came up out of the hole.

They put the ladder back in the van.

'Who found the leak?' asked Patrick.

'Er . . . I think I did,' said Ermintrude.

'Then you get the reward,' said Patrick.

'Definitely,' said Francis. And they handed Ermintrude two million pounds and drove off.

'Oh, Ermintrude, you are clever,' said Florence. 'Now we can buy the garden.'

'Do you think there'll be enough for a new hat?' said Ermintrude.

'Definitely,' they said.

Temporary fault

It was raining and everyone was at Dougal's place watching the television; everyone, that is, except Mr MacHenry and Mr Rusty and Zebedee. Mr MacHenry always took advantage of rainy days to mulch a few plants. Mr Rusty didn't care for television and Zebedee always seemed to have seen the programmes before anyway. But the others were watching.

'Don't they have a lot of programmes about dogs?' said Brian, brightly.

'Don't they, dear thing,' murmured Ermintrude.

'And what's wrong with programmes about dogs?' demanded Dougal. 'Have you got something against dogs?'

'Of course we haven't, dear heart,' said Ermintrude.

'We just mentioned it,' said Brian.

'That's all right then,' said Dougal.

'Grotty, hairy creatures,' muttered Brian.

'What?' said Dougal.

'Pretty fairy features,' said Brian, innocently.

'Watch it, snail,' said Dougal.

'Now be quiet, you two,' said Florence. The programme came to an end. An announcer appeared.

'Here is an announcement,' he said. 'We announcers are going on strike. We're fed up with all these programmes about dogs and until we get programmes that we like, we're not going to announce anything any more and that means no programmes until further notice, so there!' The screen went black. Everyone sat in stunned silence.

'What a strange thing,' said Florence.

'How odd,' said Ermintrude.

'It's an outrage!' shouted Dougal.

'It's all those dogs,' muttered Brian.

Zebedee arrived.

'Heard the news?' he asked.

'How can we?' said Dougal, tetchily, 'they've all gone on strike.'

'That's what I meant,' said Zebedee. 'Have you heard the news about the television being on strike?'

'We've just heard,' said Florence. 'Isn't it *awful*?'

'What are we going to *do*?' moaned Dougal. 'We shall miss all the weather forecasts—not to mention "Watch with Mother".'

'And all those dog programmes,' muttered Brian.

'Well, you'll just have to do something about it,' said Zebedee.

'What?' said Florence.

'One of you will have to announce the programmes,' said Zebedee.

'What?' said Florence.

'One of you will have to announce the programmes,' said Zebedee; and he left. They looked at each other.

'Crumbs,' said Brian. 'I never thought I'd be a television announcer.'

'Neither did I,' said Florence.

'Nor me,' said Ermintrude.

'Now wait just a little tiny moment!' roared Dougal. 'What makes you think you're going to be the announcers?'

'Yes, what . . . like . . . what?' said Dylan. 'What about me?'

'I don't think we can have an *American* announcing on *British* television,' murmured Florence. 'What is needed, surely, is a cultured English lady.'

'What about a cultured Scottish dog?' said Dougal.

'Or a cultured snail,' said Brian.

'Or a cultured cow?' said Ermintrude.

They all glared at each other. It was a very nasty moment. Luckily Mr Rusty came along. 'You're all looking very glary,' he said. 'Anything the matter?' So they explained

about the television announcers' strike and how Zebedee had said one of them should do it and how difficult it was to choose which one.

'Yes, I see the problem,' said Mr Rusty, 'but I also see a way out of it.'

'What?' they asked.

'Have a competition to see who's best,' said Mr Rusty. 'I'll judge it—I'm very good at judging things.'

So that's what they decided to do. Mr Rusty cut a hole in a large sheet of cardboard just like the screen of a television set and fixed it upright on the ground.

'Now you each go behind that and announce something,' he said, 'and the one who is best will win. Who wants to be first?' No one seemed very willing. Now that they were faced with the actual announcing it didn't seem such an easy job after all.

'Er . . . would you like to go first, Ermintrude?' said Florence.

'Oh, all right,' said Ermintrude. 'I can see if I don't we'll never get *anywhere*.' She went behind the screen and looked through. 'Good morning ladies and gentlemen and dogs and everyone,' she said. 'Er . . . drink more milk. Er . . . support your local cow . . . er . . . er . . . Moooo!!' She poked her head right through the hole. 'How was that?' she asked.

'Very good, Ermintrude,' said Florence.

'Next,' said Mr Rusty.

'Go on, Brian,' said Florence. Brian went behind the screen. Unfortunately Mr Rusty had made the hole rather high up and all that could be seen of Brian were his horns.

'Er . . . good morning, many and varied viewers,' he said. Dougal started to laugh. He rolled about on the ground chortling with glee.

'Er . . . can I have silence, please?' said Brian sternly from behind the screen.

'The invisible announcer!' screeched Dougal. 'Normal services will be resumed when he finds a chair to stand on! Oh dear, oh dear!' And he laughed so much he banged up against a tree and dislodged a pile of leaves over himself.

'Rotten toad,' shouted Brian. 'It's not fair! I'm not being given a fair chance. Rotters!!' And he jumped up and down behind the screen trying to be seen. This made *everyone* laugh.

'Thank you, Brian, we'll let you know,' they giggled, and Brian was so furious he rolled up into his shell and refused to come out.

'Now that wasn't very fair of you all,' said Mr Rusty, sternly, 'and I shall take that into account in the judging. Next.'

'I think Dougal should be next,' said Florence. 'Dougal!' They looked around. Dougal was nowhere to be seen.

'Where's he gone?' said Ermintrude.

'He'll miss his turn,' said Florence.

'Serve him right,' muttered Brian from inside his shell.

'Dougal!' shouted Florence. 'Dougal!'

A pile of leaves started to shake.

'Gracious, whatever's *that*?' said
Ermintrude, nervously. The pile of leaves
shook some more and started to move towards
the screen.

Brian looked out of his shell. 'What's that
pile of leaves doing?' he asked. 'We can't have a
pile of leaves as an announcer. It would be
folly.'

Just then the leaves gave a great shake and
Dougal appeared, still laughing. 'It's *me*,' he
said.

'Disguises are not allowed,' said Brian. 'You
have to appear as yourself.'

'Oh, be quiet,' giggled Dougal and he went behind the screen to make his announcement. Unfortunately he didn't realize that a lot of leaves were still stuck on his head. This made him look rather odd and everyone began to laugh, Brian most of all.

'Ladies and gentlemen,' began Dougal. 'LADIES AND GENTLEMEN!! Be quiet and listen !!' But they couldn't be quiet, not with the sight of the leaves on Dougal's head.

'Are you moulting, dear boy?' hooted Ermintrude.

'Take your hat off!' screeched Brian, while Florence and Dylan fell about laughing.

Dougal glared at them all. 'I'll report you all to the BBC,' he shouted. 'I have friends in high places!!'

'You've got leaves in high places!' shrieked Brian. 'Why don't you take your leaf?!' And he laughed so much he fell over and couldn't get up again.

Mr Rusty finally restored order by removing the leaves from Dougal's head. 'Now, be serious,' he said to him.

'I *am* being serious!' screamed Dougal. 'It's that lot there!'

'Steady, Dougal,' said Florence.

And with a lot of grumbling Dougal got on with his announcement.

'Good morning,' he announced. 'In a few minutes we shall see a very popular and entertaining documentary, "Dogs down the Ages". After that "Man's Best Friend", a study in depth of . . . er . . . the dog. This will be followed by the news.'

'Of dogs, we presume?' said Brian, sarcastically.

'Why not?' said Dougal, leaning forward through the screen, menacingly.

'What about snails?' said Brian. 'They deserve some coverage.'

'If you insist,' said Dougal, and he leapt through the screen and pushed Brian under the pile of leaves. 'Now you're covered,' he said, giggling.

'Rotter.'   Squeaked Brian.

'Now, Dougal,' said Florence, 'this is supposed to be a serious attempt to find an announcer. How can we do it if you two keep fighting all the time?'

'I'm not fighting,' said Dougal, innocently. 'I'm just covering a snail with leaves. That's not fighting, that's a public service.'

'Uncover Brian at once,' said Florence, sternly.

'Oh, fuss, fuss!' said Dougal, pushing the leaves aside. 'Come out, snail!' There was no answer from Brian.

'He's disappeared!' whispered Florence.

'Where can he have gone?' said Ermintrude.

'But he was *there*!' said Dougal. 'We all saw him!' They searched and called for Brian everywhere but they couldn't find him. It was very mysterious.

'Oh, he'll turn up,' said Dougal at last, 'he always does.' They went back to Dougal's place and had some tea, but as it got dark everyone became more and more worried about Brian.

'Perhaps I'd better see Zebedee,' said Florence.

Dylan turned the television on. 'That's no good,' said Dougal, 'it's on strike.'

But there *was* a picture on the television and as it got clearer they heard a voice saying, 'The disappearance of that very popular snail, Brian, was still being investigated tonight. Interpol has been alerted. It is thought a large ransom may be asked by an international gang.'

'I know that voice,' said Dougal, suspiciously. The picture got clearer and clearer.

'It's *Brian*!' said Florence. And it was.

'Here is an announcement,' said Brian from the television screen. 'All dog programmes have been suspended indefinitely and there now follows a three-hour documentary on the life habits and loveliness of the common or garden snail.'

'Come out!' screeched Dougal, going very close to the television.

'Sitting too close to your television set is bad for your eyes,' said Brian.

There was a knock on the door. Florence opened it. Brian came in very quietly. Everyone watched him as he went up behind Dougal, who was still shouting at the picture of Brian on the television.

'COME OUT! WE KNOW YOU'RE IN THERE!'

'He can't hear you,' said Brian quietly.
Dougal jumped round. 'What!' he said.
'What?! What?!' He looked at the picture of
Brian on the television—then he looked at
Brian behind him. He fainted.

'It's all been too much for him I think,' said Ermintrude.

Dylan fanned Dougal with a table-cloth. He came round slowly and looked at Brian. 'Snail,' he said quietly, 'don't *say* anything. Don't *do* anything. Don't make a *move*. Just tell me how you got into that television.'

BONG!!

Zebedee arrived, laughing like anything.

'Oh, I *see*,' said Dougal, heavily.

'Well, I think television always needs a little magic to help it, don't you?' said Zebedee. And everyone agreed.

Climb every mountain

One day, everyone was at Dougal's place reading books and generally sitting about, when Brian gave a shout. 'Hey, listen!' he said.

'What is it, Brian?' asked Florence.

'Yes, what is it?' said Dougal. 'Got an ant in your shell?'

'No, *listen*,' said Brian. 'It's this book. It's great.'

'What's it about, small thing?' asked Ermintrude.

'Mountains,' said Brian.

'Mountains?' said Florence.

'*Huge* mountains,' said Brian, 'and I've been thinking . . .'

'That'll be the day,' sniggered Dougal.

'Be quiet, Dougal,' said Florence. And she

asked Brian politely what was so special in the book about mountains.

'It's not what's in the book,' said Brian. 'It's just . . . well . . . mountains.'

'Yes?' they said.

'Well, we've never climbed one,' said Brian. There was a silence.

'We haven't sailed across the Atlantic either,' said Dougal.

'I was coming to that,' said Brian.

'Oh, you're hopeless,' said Dougal.

'No, Dougal, be quiet,' said Florence, and she asked Brian what was on his mind.

'Adventure,' said Brian. 'We should go in for more adventure. We should climb mountains and sail seas and explore and . . . and . . . that.'

'Go on then,' jeered Dougal, 'no one's stopping you!'

'Dougal, be quiet!' said Florence, severely, and she told Brian that she agreed with him, but it was a little difficult to climb mountains when there weren't any mountains to climb.

'So what do you say to that, boot-face?' said Dougal.

'All right,' said Brian. 'All right! You can laugh but I'm going to find a mountain and I'm going to climb it and I'll be famous and you'll all be sorry, so there.' And he trundled off in a huff.

'Oh dear, I think we've upset him,' said
Florence. 'Dougal, go and tell him we didn't
mean it.'

'Oh, he's all right,' said Dougal, 'leave him
alone.' So they all settled down to read again.
But not for long . . .

LEFT! RIGHT! LEFT! RIGHT!

'What on earth's that?' said Florence.

LEFT! RIGHT! LEFT! RIGHT!

'Sounds like an army,' said Ermintrude.

LEFT! RIGHT! LEFT! RIGHT!

Round the corner came a most extraordinary
sight. First there was Brian with a huge
rucksack on his shell and a big pair of boots
round his neck. He was carrying a banner
which read: 'EVEREST OR BUST'. Behind
him was a line of ants carrying big bundles
and, right at the end, a goat with a coil of
rope round his horns.

'Well I never!' exclaimed Florence.

'HALT!' shouted Brian, and the ants and the goat halted.

Dougal went up to Brian. 'Going fishing?' he asked.

'You may well scoff,' said Brian. 'You may scoff but this is the BRIAN expedition to Everest. I am going to plant the flag.'

Dougal laughed. The goat ambled over. 'Vat are you laffing at?' he asked. He had a strong German accent and very big horns.

'What?' said Dougal. 'What? Laughing? Who's laughing? I'm not laughing.'

'May I introduce Hans?' said Brian. 'He's going to help me climb a mountain. He's a mountain goat.'

'What's that on his horns—his knitting?' giggled Dougal.

'VAT?!' said Hans.

'Nothing,' said Dougal.

'Now,' said Brian, 'anyone who wants to join the expedition is welcome to do so but I suggest you all get your woollies and big boots. I've got mine,' he added.

'One question,' said Dougal.

'Yes?' said Brian.

'Why boots?' said Dougal.

'Can't climb mountains without proper

boots,' said Brian. 'It's a well-known fact.'

'One more question,' said Dougal.

'Yes,' said Brian.

'Where are you going to wear them?'

Brian thought.

'Oh dear,' he said.

Dougal gave a great laugh and bumped
Brian with his head. 'GREAT OAF!'
he shouted. 'WHAT ARE YOU?'

'HANS!!' screeched Brian.

Hans came over. 'Are you annoying our
leader?' he asked Dougal, lowering his horns in
a menacing fashion.

Dougal backed away. 'Of course not,' he
said, hastily. 'Why should I? He's a great
leader.' And he got behind Ermintrude and
giggled a lot.

'RIGHT!' said Brian. 'Anyone who is coming on the expedition fall in behind me.'

'FALL IN!'

'I suppose we'd better go,' murmured Florence. 'Come along.' So Ermintrude, Florence and Dougal fell in behind Brian.

'What about Dylan?' said Ermintrude.

'We'll never get him awake,' said Dougal. 'Leave him.'

'Yes, leave him at base camp,' shouted Brian.

'*Base camp?*' said Dougal.

'That's here,' said Brian. 'On! On! Forward, MARCH!!'

The expedition started off. Brian was in the lead with his banner, then came the ants, then Dougal, Florence and Ermintrude, and finally Hans.

'Have you any idea where we're going?' whispered Dougal to Florence.

'No,' said Florence.

'No whispering in the ranks!' shouted Brian.

'Oh, get off!' shouted Dougal.

'VAT?' said Hans.

'Nothing,' said Dougal. He looked at Florence. 'It's worse than being in the army,' he muttered.

'Were you ever in the army?' said Florence.

'No,' said Dougal, 'but I'm sure it's worse.'

They walked quite a long way with the ants singing a marching song at the tops of their voices.

'HALT!' said Brian at last.

Everyone halted.

'We're there,' said Brian. 'MAKE CAMP!'

Dougal, Florence and Ermintrude looked around. There were no big mountains to be seen—not even a little hill.

'Er . . . small creature,' said Ermintrude to Brian. 'I hope you don't mind my asking, but what are you going to climb?'

'You,' said Brian. There was a long silence.

'Ermintrude?' said Florence.

'*Mount* Ermintrude,' said Brian. 'Never been done before. I shall be first.'

'Have you asked permission?' said Florence, faintly.

Ermintrude started to shake with laughter.

'Permission!' she wheezed. 'Asked permission?!' She shook and shook.

'You're going to have trouble on the South Col,' giggled Dougal, looking at Ermintrude shaking.

'SILENCE!!' shouted Brian.

He turned to Ermintrude.

'I shall have to trouble you to stay still,

madam,' he said sternly. 'This is a serious expedition.'

'I'm *so* sorry,' said Ermintrude. '*Do* forgive me. Shall I take my hat off?'

'Certainly not,' said Brian. 'That's the summit.'

'You won't mind if we just watch, will you Brian?' said Florence.

'Certainly not,' said Brian, loftily. 'You can take notes and pictures and report it back to the world.'

'May I ask one more question?' said Dougal.

'Yes,' said Brian.

'Why did we have to come all this way?' said Dougal.

'Can't climb a mountain on your own doorstep,' said Brian, severely. 'It's not done.'

'Of course. Stupid of me,' said Dougal and he settled down with Florence to watch the assault on Mount Ermintrude.

Brian and Hans discussed the problem. They walked around Ermintrude pointing to various features and arguing as to the best way to go. This made Ermintrude a little nervous. 'Would it help if I sat down, dear heart?' she enquired.

'Certainly not,' said Brian. 'Mountains don't sit down.'

44

'Sorry,' said Ermintrude, 'but I've never been climbed before and you're making me nervous.'

'Mountains don't get nervous either,' said Brian, sternly.

'I'm so sorry,' said Ermintrude.

'I think ve make der assault from here,' said Hans, pointing to one of Ermintrude's back legs.

'Right,' said Brian. 'Uncoil the rope,' and he gave a piercing whistle. The ants all got up and one by one, carrying the rope between them, they began to climb up Ermintrude's leg.

'I hope she's not ticklish,' whispered Dougal.

'So do I,' said Florence. The leading ant reached Ermintrude's back, carrying the end of the rope.

'Tie it on to something!' shouted Brian.

'There's nothing to tie it on to,' squeaked the ant.

'Hammer a spike in!' shouted Hans.

'Don't you dare!!' said Ermintrude. 'I don't mind being a mountain but I will not have spikes hammered into me. Whatever next!'

'Difficult mountain,' said Brian to Hans.

'Very,' said Hans. So it was decided that all the ants should get on to Ermintrude's back and pull Brian up on the rope.

'Ready?' said Hans, tying the rope round Brian.

'Ready,' said Brian, and the ants started to pull.

'You're not climbing!' shouted Dougal. 'It's not fair!'

'I think we should keep out of this, Dougal,' whispered Florence.

Brian swayed up and up.

'Oh dear,' said Ermintrude. 'I think I'm going to sneeze!'

'No, don't!' shouted Brian. 'Mountains don't sneeze.'

'I can't stop!' said Ermintrude and with a shattering noise she gave a great sneeze.

All the ants fell over backwards and Brian was swung like a pendulum right underneath Ermintrude and up the other side, landing upside down on her head.

'HE'S MADE IT!' screeched Dougal, laughing like anything. 'I'VE MADE IT!' shouted Brian, waving his banner.

All the ants cheered and Ermintrude gave a little 'moo'. 'I may have to sit down,' she said. 'I feel a little faint.' And she sat down. As she did so all the ants and Brian slithered down her back and on to the ground.

'AVALANCHE!' hooted Dougal. Brian and the ants picked themselves up.

'I think we can say that was a success,' said Brian, modestly.

'I expect you'd all like some tea?' said Florence, trying not to laugh.

'TEA FOR ALL!' screeched Dougal.

'TEA FOR ALL!' chorused the ants.

Ermintrude got up. 'What an experience,' she said, and they all set off back to Dougal's place for tea.

'Tell me something, Brian,' said Florence. 'Why did you want to climb Ermintrude?'

'Because she was there,' said Brian happily.

Seaside

There was great excitement in the garden. Everyone was going on a trip to the seaside in the train. It was Mr Rusty's idea. He and Mr MacHenry had once spent a very enjoyable time at Bournemouth and they wanted to do it again. There was one slight snag. The train wasn't sure how to get to Bournemouth and so wasn't making any promises.

'Well, it doesn't *have* to be Bournemouth,' said Dougal.

'Very pretty, Bournemouth,' said Mr Rusty.

'Well, so's Brighton,' said Dougal.

'And Bognor,' said Florence.

'And Ramsgate,' said Ermintrude.

'And Oldham,' said Brian. They looked at him.

'I don't think Oldham is by the sea, Brian,' said Florence.

'Oh, have they moved it?' said Brian.

'Really,' said Dougal. 'Don't you know *anything?*'

'I know Oldham,' said Brian. 'Oldham-on-Sea, that is . . .'

'Ignore him,' said Dougal. So they ignored

Brian and started making plans.
'You're ignoring me,'
said Brian, but no one
took any notice.

'Now,' said Florence. 'We shall all need a
bathing-suit and a towel and I think we should
take a picnic as well, in case.'

'In basket,' said Brian.

'I beg your pardon?' said Florence.

'You take a picnic in a basket, not a case,'
said Brian.

'Oh, ignore him,' said Dougal, heavily. So
they ignored Brian again and started to get
their things together.

Ermintrude's bathing-costume was huge and covered with big flowers. Dougal's was rather old-fashioned with a lot of stripes and Florence's was a very elegant two-piece.

'Where's your costume, snail?' said Dougal.

'Snails don't need costumes,' said Brian, loftily. 'Unlike soggy doggies, snails are waterproof.'

'Are they thump-proof?' asked Dougal.

'That's enough, Dougal,' said Florence, and she told Brian that he ought to have a bathing-costume, especially if they were going to Bournemouth.

'I'll wear my water-wings,' said Brian, and he rummaged about in his shell and produced a pair of huge water-wings which he blew up with a great deal of noisy effort.

'Everyone ready?' said Ermintrude, 'because I think the train is coming.'

'HELP!' shouted Brian suddenly. 'HELP! HELP!' Everyone looked as Brian rose slowly into the air supported by his huge water-wings.

'SAVE ME!' squeaked Brian.

'Anyone got an air-gun?' asked Dougal, evilly. Brian got higher and higher and began to float away over the trees.

'Oh dear,' said Florence. But luckily the top branch of one tree was just slightly higher than all the others and Brian caught on it.

'EEK!' he shrieked. 'GET ME DOWN!'

The train arrived. 'Everyone ready?' she asked. 'Because we haven't got all day. (I've got to be at Watford for a reunion after I've delivered you lot.)'

'Well,' said Florence, 'we are *nearly* all ready. It's just Brian.'

'He's up a tree,' said Dougal.

'Up a tree?' said the train. 'What's he doing up a tree?'

'Trying out his water-wings,' giggled Dougal. Everyone got in the train and they steamed over to Brian's tree.

'Come down!' said the train. 'I'm behind schedule.'

'*I'm* up a tree,' wailed Brian.

Mr Rusty had an idea. Why not tell Brian to let some air out of his water-wings and float down? This seemed to be a good idea and they suggested it to Brian. Brian tried it and floated down—straight into the engine's funnel.

'GED OUD OB DERE,' shouted the train, and she gave a great sneeze.

Brian hurtled out of the funnel and landed

with a thump on the ground. He was covered
in soot and very cross. 'Oh, I'm so *cross!*' he
squeaked.

'Oh, get in,' said Dougal, 'and stop playing about.' So Brian got in, muttering a lot and spraying soot all over everything.

'I hope you're not going into the sea like that,' said Dougal. 'You'll pollute the whole south coast.' But Florence cleaned Brian up with her handkerchief and they finally set out for a destination somewhere by the seaside.

'Oh, isn't it pretty?' said Florence when they arrived.

'Is it Bournemouth?' asked Mr Rusty, anxiously. They looked around.

'There's a notice board over there, man,' said Dylan, yawning. So they all got out of the train and went to look. 'OLDHAM-ON-SEA WELCOMES CAREFUL BATHERS,' it said. Brian looked very smug.

'Oh, he'll be impossible all day now,' groaned Dougal. But Florence said it didn't matter where they were as long as they had a good time and, telling the train to expect them back at about six o'clock, they all set out for the beach. They didn't reach it. Dougal and Brian had found another notice. It said:

AMUSEMENTS!! FUN!! LAUGHTER!!
RIDE THE BIG WHEEL!!
DODGE THE DODGEMS!!
SEE THE FAT LADY!!

'Cor!' said Brian. 'Let's go in here!'

'Oh, Brian,' said Florence, 'don't you want a swim and a sunbathe?'

'Not 'til I've seen the fat lady,' said Brian. 'I've never seen a fat lady.'

'What are you looking at me for, dear thing?' said Ermintrude, sharply.

'Come on, let's go in,' said Dougal.

'Well, just for five minutes,' sighed Florence.

Mr MacHenry and Mr Rusty said they were a bit too old for amusements and *they* were going to have a paddle. 'We'll see you on the beach later,' they said.

Dougal, Brian, Ermintrude, Dylan and Florence went into the amusement park. There were swings and roundabouts and big wheels and dodgem cars and roll-a-penny stalls and darts stalls and bow and arrow stalls and all sorts of things.

'Anyone want to go on the roundabout?' asked Florence.

'I think we've had enough of that at home,' said Dougal.

They went on the dodgem cars. Dougal and Brian in one, Florence and Dylan in another and Ermintrude in one by herself. Dougal and Brian argued about who was to steer.

'I'm a great little steerer,' said Brian.

'What do you use, your nose?' asked Dougal.

CRASH! Ermintrude had rammed them from behind. Dougal fell upside-down in a heap on the seat and Brian clung to the wheel, shrieking.

'Sorry, dear hearts!' said Ermintrude.

'You're supposed to *dodge!*' roared Dougal.

'What fun is *that!*' said Ermintrude, and aimed for them again.

'Look out!' shouted Dougal, and Brian swung the steering-wheel round and headed straight for the side. CRASH!! The car hit the side, bounced over and started to rush very fast through the fairground.

'WHEEE!!' shouted Brian. 'WHEEEE!!!'

'Stop it, you mad mollusc!' screeched Dougal.

They went through the flap of a tent and out the other side carrying with them a very fat lady. 'Now boys!' she said. 'That's enough! You haven't paid!'

'Put her back!' shrieked Dougal, but Brian
paid no attention. They drove in and out of
stalls, scattering coconuts and china dogs in all
directions.

'Ooo!' moaned the fat lady, clinging to
Dougal. 'I don't feel very well.'

'Please, madam,' said Dougal, 'try to control
yourself.'

Brian headed the car back towards the
dodgem ring. 'Look out, here we come!'
he shouted, and with a crash they were back
whizzing around after Ermintrude.

'Dougal, what are you doing?!' said Florence
as they rushed by.

'Me?!' said Dougal. 'I'm not doing
anything. It's this demented snail.'

'WHEE!!' shouted Brian. 'Wheee!!
Wheee!! Wheeeeeee . . .'

The cars slowed down and finally stopped.
The fat lady got up off Dougal. 'Thanks for the
ride, boys,' she said, patting her hair into place.
'Come up and see me sometime.' And she left.

'What shall we do now?' said Brian,
excitedly. 'Can we see the fat lady?'

'I've seen enough fat ladies to last me a
life-time,' said Dougal, heavily. 'And I'll
trouble you to keep out of my way for a little
while.'

'Why, what have I done?' asked Brian, innocently.

They collected Dylan, who had fallen asleep, and wandered round the fairground. 'GHOST TRAIN' said a notice. There were pictures of ghosts and skulls and other very nasty things painted everywhere. 'Er . . . want to go on?' said Florence.

'Cor, yes!' said Brian. 'Come on! I love a ghostie!' The others weren't too sure.

'I'll only go if I can sit in the middle,' said Ermintrude, nervously.

'Come on!' said Brian, so they all got on.

The train moved forward very slowly, pushed its way through some doors into total darkness, and then started to go very fast.

'If you say "*Whee!*", snail,' said Dougal, 'I shall strike you.'

'WHEEE!!' came a loud screech.

'It wasn't me!' said Brian hastily.

They hurtled through. Skeletons and flapping sheets and glaring eyes rushed at them. Florence kept her eyes firmly shut and Dougal put his head under the seat. Only Brian seemed to be enjoying himself. He screeched back at the ghosts and stuck his tongue out at the skeletons. They came out into the light again and got off. Dougal was shaking and Florence still had her eyes closed.

'Where's Ermintrude?' said Brian. They looked. Ermintrude wasn't on the train.

'The ghosties got her,' whispered Brian.

'Oh, be quiet!' said Dougal.

Florence went up to the doors very bravely and called, 'Ermintrude!' There was a 'moo' from inside. It got louder and louder and another train rushed out of the tunnel with Ermintrude on the front. She looked very white and was shaking all over. Her hat had slipped over one eye and she had great difficulty walking.

'What happened?' said Florence.

Ermintrude pulled herself together with an effort. 'My dears,' she said, 'I'm *so* sorry, but I forgot where I was. I had my eyes shut and I knew I was on a train, so I thought I'd go to the buffet car for a glass of milk to make me feel better.'

'Oh dear,' said Florence.

'Yes,' said Ermintrude, with feeling. 'I've been rushing about in there like a feather in the breeze.'

'Some feather,' muttered Dougal.

Florence suggested that perhaps everyone had had enough excitement for one day so they decided to get Mr Rusty and Mr MacHenry and all go home. On the beach there was no sign of either Mr Rusty or Mr MacHenry.

'I expect they've gone back to the train,' said Florence. But suddenly there was a loud snore from underneath a pile of deckchairs. They looked. There were Mr Rusty and Mr MacHenry fast asleep.

'Had a good sunbathe?' shouted Dougal. Mr Rusty and Mr MacHenry crawled out.

'Oh, I feel better for that,' said Mr Rusty.

'Just like Bournemouth,' said Mr MacHenry.

'I don't know why we bothered to bring them,' whispered Dougal.

'Well at least they're not . . . like . . . exhausted,' yawned Dylan.

'I like *that*,' said Dougal. 'You haven't said or done anything all day!'

'No, but I've thought a lot,' said Dylan.

'Home we go,' said Florence, and home they went.

On the farm

One day, Mr MacHenry told everyone he had
arranged for them to visit a friend of his who
had a farm. 'Do you all good, a day in the
country,' he said.

'We're *always* in the country,' said Dougal.
'We *live* in the country. How about a trip to
London?'

'We can do that another day, Dougal,' said
Florence. 'I'd like to go to a farm.'

Dougal sighed. 'I can see trouble ahead,'
he said, 'squelching through mud, falling into
ditches, being chased by mad bulls . . .'

'Really?!!' said Ermintrude, eagerly.

'I don't want to be chased by a mad bull,' said Brian nervously. 'It might catch me.'

'We should be so lucky,' muttered Dougal.

'How are we going to get there?' said Dylan.

'We're being *fetched*,' said Mr MacHenry.

'Rolls-Royce?' said Dougal.

'Bus?' said Brian.

'Golden Coach?' said Florence.

'Cart and tractor,' said Mr MacHenry.

'CART?!' said Dougal.

'TRACTOR?!' said Brian.

'Yes, and here it comes,' said Mr MacHenry. A huge red tractor pulling a big cart came into the garden. Driving it was a very large lady in a wide-brimmed hat.

'Good morning, Mr MacHenry,' she said.

'Good morning, Miss Pennyquick,' said Mr MacHenry. 'They're all here.' Brian prodded Dylan, who had fallen asleep, and they all got into the cart and said good-bye to Mr MacHenry.

'Lots of sacks to sit on,' shouted Miss Pennyquick. 'Make yourselves comfortable.'

'Isn't this exciting?' said Florence.

'Ecstatic,' groaned Dougal, looking for a place to sit. 'Move up, snail.'

'I can't,' hissed Brian. 'There's a cow in the

way.'

'Oh sorry, dear heart. Am I taking up too much room?' said Ermintrude. Truth to tell, Ermintrude *was* taking up rather a lot of room—everyone was squashed towards the back of the cart, and as Miss Pennyquick put the tractor into gear and started, Ermintrude slid backwards and squashed them even more.

'Er . . . Ermintrude,' said Florence, 'could you possibly ease up a little?'

'Just a tidge,' squeaked Brian.

'Like about six feet?' said Dougal. Ermintrude eased up and everyone made themselves as comfortable as they could. The tractor went through a gate and started across a ploughed field. It was rather bumpy.

'I may never survive this,' sighed Dougal.

'Smell the country air,' squeaked Brian.

'Deep breaths!' said Florence.

'I'm finding it difficult to take any sort of breath,' said Dougal, grumpily, bouncing up and down.

'Oh, stop grumping, Dougal,' said Florence. They went through a gate into a wood.

'HEADS DOWN!' shouted Miss Pennyquick.

'What?' said Dougal, standing up. A low branch caught him and lifted him straight out of the cart. 'HELP!' he shrieked. 'Wait for me!'

'Come on, Dougal,' said Florence. 'Catch us up!'

Dougal ran after the cart, squelching through the mud. 'I told you! I told you!' he screeched.

'I told you it would be squelching through mud and falling . . .' He disappeared.

'Into ditches,' said Brian, giggling.

They stopped and waited for Dougal, who climbed back on board very muddy and very grumpy.

'Invigorating, isn't it?' said Brian, brightly. Dougal sat on him.

'Now, Dougal,' said Florence, 'get off Brian and stop being grumpy.'

'I told you!' muttered Dougal, getting off Brian.

'He's always sitting on me!' said Brian. 'It's not fair!'

'Well, you shouldn't upset him,' said Florence, severely.

'*Anything* upsets *him*,' said Brian, wiping mud off his nose on to Dougal.

'Don't wipe yourself on me!' roared Dougal.

'Now listen!' said Florence. 'Any more of this and we'll all go straight home.'

'Promise?' said Dougal, and he and Brian fell about, giggling.

'What a pair,' murmured Ermintrude. 'What a pair!'

They arrived at the farm and stopped. 'Everyone out,' said Miss Pennyquick, 'and I'll show you round.' Everyone got out except

Dylan who had fallen asleep again under a
pile of sacks, and started on a tour of
inspection with Miss Pennyquick.

'This is the main yard,' she said, 'and that's
my house over there.' She pointed. The house
had roses round the door and ivy growing up
the walls.

'Oh, isn't that pretty?' breathed Florence.

'Reminds me of home,' sniffed Ermintrude.

'Sentimental pair,' whispered Dougal to Brian. 'Ooo isn't it pretty!!' he simpered.

'Reminds me of home!' said Brian, pretending to cry a lot. They shrieked with laughter and clung on to each other.

'I trust you are not making fun of me?' said Ermintrude, towering over them.

'Or me?' said Florence.

'Oh no, certainly not,' they said, trying not to laugh.

'We're glad,' said Ermintrude and Florence.

'Come along everyone,' said Miss Pennyquick. 'We'll go and see the hens.' They went across the yard and through a little gate beside a barn. There was an enormous hen-run full of speckly hens.

'Oh, what a lot,' said Florence, as the hens crowded round. 'Do they lay well?'

'Best in the country,' said Miss Pennyquick. 'You three go into the hen-house and get some eggs while Ermintrude and I put the kettle on.' Dougal, Brian and Florence crossed to the hen-house and went inside. It was rather dark.

'Could someone put the light on?' said Brian nervously.

'DON'T YOU DARE PUT A LIGHT ON!' said a voice, very loudly.

Dougal jumped. 'Who was *that*?' he asked.

'I don't know,' said Florence.

'It was *me*,' said the voice, crossly. When their eyes got used to the darkness they saw it was a very large hen sitting on a nest, knitting a long scarf.

'Er . . . we've come for some eggs,' said Florence, nervously.

'Have you, dear?' said the hen. 'Well, help yourself.' Florence went to some of the nesting-boxes and collected a few eggs.

'Thank you,' she said, 'come along you two.'

But Dougal and Brian wanted to collect a few eggs too. 'We'll be along later,' they said, so Florence left.

The large hen eyed Dougal and Brian.

'What are you two up to?' she said, suspiciously.

'Nothing,' they said, innocently.

Dougal got a basket from a hook on the wall, Brian climbed up into a nesting-box and rolled an egg out. It missed the basket and hit Dougal on the head. 'Clumsy oaf!' he screeched, and he started to chase Brian round the hen-house.

'STOP IT!' said the speckled hen.

'STOP IT!' said the other hens, popping their heads out of boxes. 'WE MUST HAVE SILENCE!' But Dougal and Brian raced round knocking into things and making a lot of noise.

'HAROLD!!' shouted the hens. The door opened. 'HAROLD! DO SOMETHING!' An enormous cockerel came in. 'Having trouble?' he asked. Dougal and Brian stopped

running. The cockerel
came towards them.
'Having fun?'
he asked, quietly.

Dougal and Brian backed away. 'Sorry, sir,'
they said, 'just collecting a few eggs, sir. Just
going, sir.'

'GIVE THEM A PECK, HAROLD!'
shouted the hens.

'That won't be necessary,' said Dougal,
hastily, and he and Brian left very hurriedly.
'Nasty moment, that,' said Dougal when they
were safely outside.

'Did you see the size of that beak?' said Brian.
They walked slowly through the crowd of

speckly hens. Suddenly, there was a great rush of wings and Harold was fluttering towards them very fast.

'RUN!' said Dougal. They raced to the gate and just got out as Harold hit it with a great crash and a flutter of feathers. Dougal and Brian ran on and reached the house, panting.

'Did you get any eggs?' said Florence.

'No, we didn't bother,' said Dougal.

'No, didn't bother,' squeaked Brian.

'Did you meet Harold?' asked Miss Pennyquick.

'Harold?' said Dougal. 'Oh yes, charming, lovely . . . er . . . cockerel . . .'

'Tea?' said Florence.

'No, thank you,' said Dougal and Brian.

'Boiled egg?' said Florence.

'Yes, please,' said Dougal and Brian.

After tea they went to look around some more. Ermintrude met a herd of cows and stopped to chat. Dougal, Brian and Florence wandered on across a field. 'What's that notice say?' asked Brian, nodding towards a board nailed to a tree.

'Go and see,' said Florence. 'I'll wait for Ermintrude.' Dougal and Brian went towards the notice board.

'Enjoying yourself, snail?' asked Dougal.

'Hugely,' said Brian. 'Are you, old agricultural mate?'

'Oh, shut up!' said Dougal. They came to the notice board.

'What's it say?' said Brian. Dougal didn't answer. He had gone quite white and rigid.

'Hey, you've gone quite white and rigid,' said Brian. 'Anything wrong?' Dougal still didn't move. Brian looked at the notice. 'BEWARE OF THE BULL', it said.

'Beware of the *ball*?' said Brian. 'What's that mean? "Beware of the *ball*". I've never heard that before.'

'B . . . b . . . b . . . b . . . ,' said Dougal.

'I beg your pardon?' said Brian.

'B . . . b . . . b . . . b . . . BULL!!' stuttered Dougal..

'Hey, steady on,' said Brian.

'BEWARE OF THE *BULL!!*' screeched Dougal. 'Not BALL, BULL!!'

Brian disappeared like lightning into his shell.

'COME OUT, COWARD!' shouted Dougal.

'Not likely,' said Brian. Dougal looked around wildly. He picked Brian up and started to run back across the field. He'd almost got to the gate when there was a snort and a stamp behind him. Dougal dropped Brian and buried his head in a tuft of grass. The snorting and stamping got louder and a huge black bull prodded Dougal with his nose.

'Eek!!' shrieked Dougal. 'Help! Go away!! Help!! Help!!'

'What on earth is going on here?' asked Ermintrude, putting her head over the gate.

'I'm being attacked!' screamed Dougal.

'So am I!' shouted Brian, from inside his shell.

Ermintrude looked at the bull. 'How *dare* you!' she said, in a very firm voice.

The bull retreated a few steps.

'I 'aven't done nuffink,' he said.

'Haven't done anything!' said Ermintrude.
'You've frightened my friends! You call that
nothing?' She opened the gate and went very
close to the big black bull. 'You should be
ashamed!' she said.

'Look 'ere,' said the bull. 'I'm supposed to be
fierce. I got a notice to prove it.'

'You, *fierce?!*' scoffed Ermintrude. 'You
couldn't knock the skin off a rice pudding.
Now go away and eat some grass.'

'Ooo . . . you are *forceful!*' said the bull.

'And don't be cheeky,' said Ermintrude,
smiling. The bull wandered off and the others
went back to the house.

'I thought you were very brave.'

'Be quiet, snail,' said Dougal, 'if you value your chances of getting home unthumped.'

'Had a good time?' said Miss Pennyquick.

'Lovely,' said Florence, 'but I think we should go now, thank you.'

They all got back into the cart and drove back to the garden.

'Where's Dylan?' said Mr MacHenry when they'd thanked Miss Pennyquick and waved good-bye.

'Oh dear,' said Florence, 'I think he was under those sacks.'

'Don't worry, the walk back will do him good,' sniggered Dougal.

'Anyone like some supper?' asked Florence. So they all had supper and there was just enough left for Dylan when he got back.

'Had a good walk?' said Dougal.

'Man,' said Dylan, with feeling, and he fell asleep.

Dougal the lion-heart

Everyone was at Florence's place early one morning having breakfast and wondering what to do.

'Pass me another piece of toast,' said Dougal, lazily. Florence passed it. 'And the butter,' said Dougal. Florence passed it. 'And the marmalade,' said Dougal. Florence passed it.

'Would you like me to eat it for you, Dougal?' she asked, icily.

'I can manage,' said Dougal.

'*Hey!*' said Brian, suddenly.

Dougal jumped.

'WHY DO YOU ALWAYS DO THAT?!'
he roared, wiping butter and marmalade
off his nose.

'No, listen,' said Brian. 'It says in the paper

here that last night a lion escaped from the circus.'

'So what, dear heart?' said Ermintrude.

'Well,' said Brian, 'you know that circus we were all going to go to?'

'Yes,' they said.

'Well that's the one,' said Brian.

'The one *what?*' they asked.

'The one the lion's escaped from,' said Brian.

They were all quiet for a moment.

'But that's very close to *here*,' said Dougal, going very pale.

'Two minutes away,' whispered Florence.

'Just round the corner,' said Brian, cheerfully. 'Pour me another cup, would you?'

'How can you think of tea at a time like this?' demanded Dougal. 'We might all be eaten in our beds.'

'We're not *in* bed,' said Brian.

'That's beside the point,' said Dougal.

'Now, Dougal,' said Florence, 'there's no need to be alarmist about this.'

'I think there's every need,' said Dougal, hotly. 'Great lions wandering about all over the place chomping things.'

'Only one, Dougal,' said Florence.

'Only *one!*' said Dougal. '*Only* one! How many do you want?'

'Perhaps we could tame him,' said Brian, 'you know, like they do.'

Dougal looked at him. 'We can call upon your lion-taming experience, I presume,' he said, witheringly.

'There's no need to be withering,' said Brian.

'Now listen,' said Florence. 'There's absolutely no need to be worried. It's probably a lovely lion.'

'And it's probably back in its cage by now, anyway,' said Ermintrude.

'And it probably won't come this way anyway,' said Brian.

'GROWWLLLL!!!!!!!'

Everyone went quite silent.

'Was that you, snail?' whispered Dougal.

'Don't be soppy,' whispered Brian.

'GROWWLLLLL!!!!!'

'I think that's it, dear things,' said Ermintrude, faintly.

'I'm too young to be eaten,' squeaked Brian.

'I'll remember to tell it that,' hissed Dougal.

'What are we going to do?' said Florence. No one seemed to know.

'Have a look out of the window, Dougal,' they said.

'Why me?' said Dougal.

'You're nearest,' they said. Dougal crept over

to the window and looked out. 'Well?' they said.

'I can't see anything,' said Dougal.

'It's gone away,' said Ermintrude.

'Have a look out of the door, Dougal,' they said.

'Why me?' said Dougal.

'You're the nearest,' they said. Dougal tiptoed over to the door and opened it a crack.

'GROWWLLLL!!!!'

Dougal slammed the door and fell over backwards.

'It's . . . it's . . . it's . . . ,' he stuttered.

'Out there?' said Brian.

'Oh dear,' said Florence, 'what *are* we going to do?' No one could offer any suggestion at all.

'We're all a bit inexperienced in this sort of thing, I'm afraid,' said Ermintrude.

'I've got an idea,' said Brian. 'Why doesn't one of us go out there and offer him a little snack while the others creep away . . . and that?' They looked at him.

'What a great idea,' said Dougal. 'Brilliant.'

'Thank you,' said Brian.

'Go on then,' said Dougal.

'What?' said Brian.

'Go out and offer him a biccy,' said Dougal.

'Me?' said Brian, faintly.

'Well you said "one of us" and you're one of us,' said Dougal.

'It wasn't quite what I had in mind,' said Brian.

'No, I bet it wasn't,' said Dougal scathingly.

Ermintrude got up. 'I'll go,' she said, going to the door.

'Oh, Ermintrude do be careful,' said Florence.

'Oh, I will, dear,' said Ermintrude, and she

went out closing the door behind her. There was silence for a moment.

'I was very fond of Ermintrude,' said Brian, sighing.

'Brian, be quiet,' said Florence, and she went to the door and listened.

'Hear anything?' said Dougal.

'Nothing,' said Florence. She opened the door a tiny crack and peeped out. She opened it wider. She went out.

'I was fond of Florence, too,' sighed Brian, sniffing.

'Oh control yourself, snail,' said Dougal.

Dylan got up from a chair where he'd been fast asleep and yawned. 'What's going on, men?' he asked.

'Nothing,' said Dougal, quickly. 'Er . . . nothing.'

'Then I think I'll go for a stroll through the cabbages,' said Dylan. 'Coming?'

'Er . . . not just now,' said Dougal, and he closed the door behind Dylan.

'Another one gone,' said Brian, mournfully.

'Only one left now.'

He gave a great sniff and a tear rolled down his cheek.

'WHAT DO YOU MEAN?!' said Dougal. 'WHAT ABOUT ME?!!'

'Oh yes,' said Brian, 'there is you.' He went up to Dougal. 'Good-bye, old chum,' he said.

'Going somewhere?' said Dougal, icily.

'No,' said Brian, 'but I thought you'd probably be popping out to see what's happened to . . . to . . . the others.'

'We'll *both* go,' said Dougal. 'Come on.'

'Oh, I feel quite wobbly,' said Brian. 'You'll have to carry me.'

'Oh, good heavens,' said Dougal. 'What a pathetic creature. Get on then.' So Brian got on to Dougal's head and they both crept out of the door into the garden.

'Isn't it quiet?' whispered Brian.

'*Too* quiet,' whispered Dougal. 'I don't like it.'

'Shall I sing?' asked Brian.

'You dare!' said Dougal. They went on. Suddenly Dougal stopped. There was Ermintrude's hat lying on the ground.

'Oh woe!' wailed Brian. 'Ermintrude! Eaten! Only her hat left! Oh, the cruel beastie! Oh woe! Woe!'

'Be quiet!' said Dougal. 'Stop jumping to conclusions. If she'd been eaten there wouldn't be just her hat left. There'd be . . .'

'What?' said Brian.

'Bits,' said Dougal.

'*Bits!!*' said Brian, going pale. 'Oh, I feel quite faint.'

'Pull yourself together,' said Dougal. They went on. There was one of Florence's shoes lying in the path.

'Eeeh!' screeched Brian. 'Another victim! Oh woe! Oh woe!'

'SILENCE!' said Dougal. 'I know what it is! They've left a trail! Come on!' And he raced along the path with Brian bumping about on

top of his head. They rounded a corner and slid
right into the side of a huge tent. Brian shot
upwards, slid back down the canvas and landed
on top of Dougal. 'Ooof!' said Dougal.

'Oh, sorry,' said Brian. 'Are you damaged?'

'Anyone would be damaged if hit by a great
fat snail,' said Dougal, huffily. 'What *is* this?'

'It's a tent,' said Brian.

'What's a tent doing in the garden?' said
Dougal.

'Perhaps it's Boy Scouts,' said Brian. He
looked at the huge expanse of canvas.

'*Big* Boy Scouts,' he added.

They went round the side of the tent and came to an opening.

'Twenty-five pence,' said a voice.

'I beg your pardon?' said Dougal to Brian.

'I didn't say anything,' said Brian.

'Twenty-five pence,' said the voice again. They looked up. There was a little man sitting in a little box. 'It's twenty-five pence,' he said. 'Each.'

'Er . . . well,' said Dougal. 'Er . . . I appear to have come without my purse. Snail,' he said, 'have you got any money?'

'Hang on,' said Brian, and he disappeared into his shell. There was a noise of chinking inside and Brian muttering to himself. He came out again. 'I had to open my piggy bank,' he said. 'Here you are.'

He gave Dougal fifty pence and Dougal gave them to the man.

'Thank you,' said the man. 'Hurry along, please.' Brian and Dougal started to go. 'Hey!' said the man. 'You're going the wrong way— through here!' He pointed to a flap in the tent. Brian and Dougal looked at each other.

'I think we've paid to enter the tent,' said Brian.

'I don't want to go in a tent,' said Dougal,

tetchily. 'I can go into tents any time.'

'HURRY ALONG!' shouted the man and Brian and Dougal were so startled, they rushed into the tent and didn't stop running until they found themselves in the centre of a huge ring and surrounded by iron bars.

There was a great cheer. Dougal and Brian looked round. They were in a circus tent and it was full of people.

'Hallo, you two!' shouted some voices. They looked again. There were Florence, Ermintrude, Dylan, Mr Rusty, Mr MacHenry and Zebedee sitting in a row watching them. Dougal looked at Brian and Brian looked at Dougal.

'It's a circus,' whispered Dougal.

'And we're in it,' whispered Brian.

'What are these iron bars?' said Dougal.

'Oh, they're just the things they put up for the lion-tamers,' said Brian.

Dougal went quite white.

'LET ME OUT!' he screeched.

'AND ME!' screeched Brian.

But it was too late. Into the ring bounded six huge lions who started circling round Brian and Dougal, snarling and roaring. Brian disappeared into his shell.

'Come out, coward!' shouted Dougal.

'I'm in the bath!' shouted Brian. The lions circled and roared. Dougal circled and squeaked.

'BACK!' he shouted. 'BACK!'

One of the lions came over to him and opened his mouth very wide.

'Er . . . good afternoon,' said Dougal. 'Er . . . lovely day.'

The lion looked at him. 'We've got a right one here,' he said to the others, and they all started leaping on to boxes and jumping over Dougal, laughing like anything.

Into the ring came a huge man dressed in very tight trousers, boots and a little vest. He carried a whip and a chair.

'What are *you* doing here?' he demanded of Dougal.

'I'm sorry,' said Dougal. 'I . . . er . . . we . . . just lost our way.'

Brian popped out of his shell. 'Have they gone?' he asked.

Dougal picked him up and rushed round and round the cage. Everyone cheered like anything and the lions couldn't stop laughing. Finally, Dougal spotted a little tunnel made of iron bars. He rushed down it and found himself outside the cage. He put Brian down. 'You can open your eyes now,' he said, sarcastically.

'You saved me!' said Brian. 'My friend! My little lion-taming mate!'

'That's enough,' said Dougal. 'Come on.'

They found Florence and the others. 'Dougal, you were wonderful,' said Florence.

'Great, man,' said Dylan.

'Stupendous,' said Ermintrude. Dougal sat down heavily. The lion-tamer was still at it in the ring and the lions were leaping and roaring.

'Why didn't you tell us you could tame lions, Dougal?' said Florence.

'You never asked me,' said Dougal.